CLAUDE
Camp Claude

BASED ON THE *Alex T. Smith* CLAUDE STORIES

DEVISED FOR TELEVISION BY *Sixteen South*

"This book I bought with my pocket money is very exciting," said Claude one morning. "It's all about living in the wild . . . finding huge insects, running from stampeding animals, swinging through trees!"

"Who on earth would ever want to do that?" Sir Bobblysock asked, horrified.

"It would be an adventure!" said Claude. "We could take a picnic.
And you could wear your safari hat!"

Well, that *did* change things a little . . .

"But who would save me," swooned Sir Bobblysock, "if something
really wild happened?"

Claude's ears wobbled and his tail waggled . . .

His eyebrows wiggled . . .

and he said —

"I CAN DO THAT!"

"Well, all right then," sighed Sir Bobblysock.
"Just as long as we can take certain provisions . . ."

"Oof! This tea set is quite heavy," said Claude.

"You can never be too prepared when you're
so far away from home," said Sir Bobblysock.

"Do you really think our back garden is wild enough?" said Claude, looking around.

"Oh, yes!" said Sir Bobblysock. "Mr and Mrs Shinyshoes have really let it go lately. Who knows what could be lurking in all that long grass. We'll have to be on our guard."

"I think it's time for a snack," said Claude.
But as soon as he had spread the picnic blanket on
the ground, Sir Bobblysock let out a scream.

"Argh!" he shrieked. "A *huge* creepy crawly!"

"Where?" said Claude.
"I can't see anything."

"There!" said Sir Bobblysock. "By the cucumber sandwiches."

Claude pulled out a magnifying glass from under his beret. "It's just an ant."

"Well, he's looking at me funny!

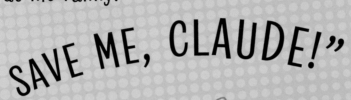

SAVE ME, CLAUDE!"

"Don't worry, Sir Bobblysock!" cried Claude.
"We can take shelter in the tent."

But then Claude got all tangled up in the tent ropes and fell over – right into the flowerbed!

"Oh no! Look what I've done to the flowers," said Claude.

"Oh dear, you *are* in a pickle. Let me help!" said Sir Bobblysock.

But he accidentally stood on a bendy tent pole that went . . .

TWANGGG!

. . . and sent him flying up,
up into the air . . .

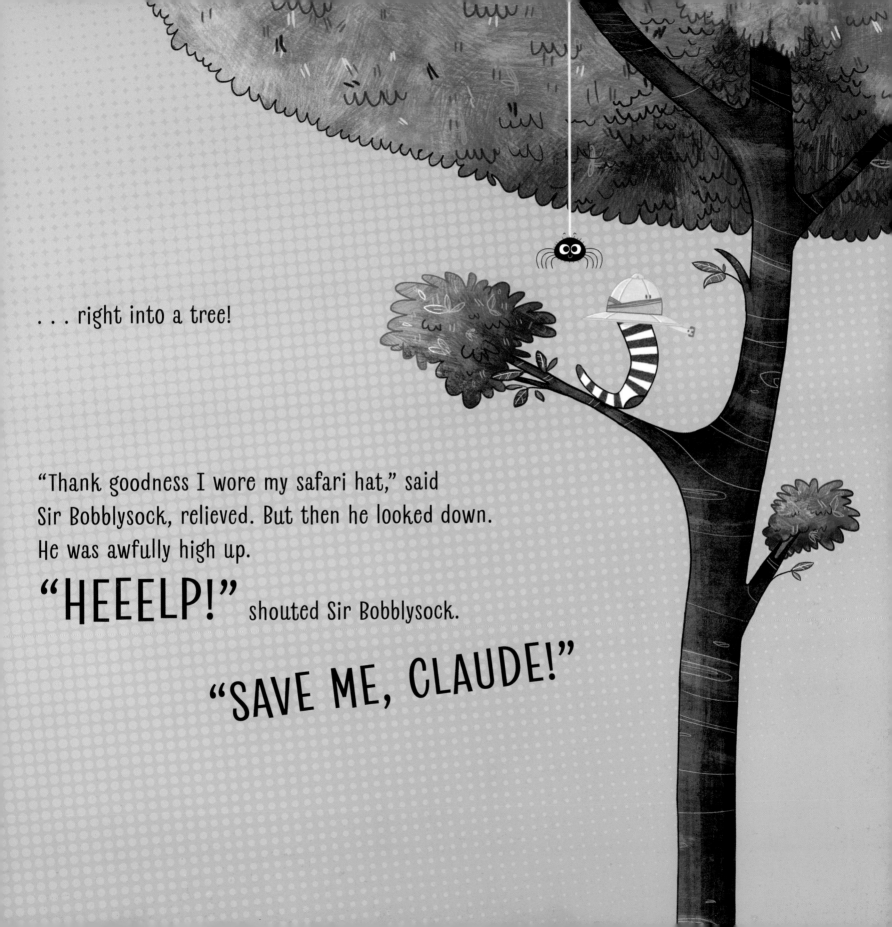

. . . right into a tree!

"Thank goodness I wore my safari hat," said
Sir Bobblysock, relieved. But then he looked down.
He was awfully high up.

"HEEELP!" shouted Sir Bobblysock.

"SAVE ME, CLAUDE!"

"Don't worry, Sir Bobblysock,"
said Claude.
"I'll get you down!"

Claude quickly put on his climbing gear
and grabbed the hose to use as a rope –
but he accidentally turned it on and . . .

SPLOSH!

. . . gave the whole garden
a good hosing down!

"Claude!" yelped Sir Bobblysock. "Less
splashing about and more rescuing, please!"

Claude turned off the hose and lassooed it to a branch. Then he climbed up the tree and brought Sir Bobblysock safely back down to earth.

"You do take care of me, Claude," said Sir Bobblysock.

"And now I'd better take care of the hose
and tidy it up," said Claude.
But as he tidied away the hosepipe,
he heard another scream . . .

"AAARRRGGGH!"

"W-w-w-wild animals!"
said Sir Bobblysock. "Save me, Claude!
Save me AGAIN!"

"They're only bunny rabbits," giggled Claude.
But he scooped Sir Bobblysock up and carried him to safety.

"My hero!" said Sir Bobblysock.
"I think it might be time to go back inside now, Claude. Don't you?"

Claude gave Sir Bobblysock an ice pack to help soothe his nerves.

"What an adventure that was," said Claude, "and all in our own back garden!"

"I do hope Mr and Mrs Shinyshoes tidy it up a bit," said Sir Bobblysock. "It's like a jungle out there."

Claude gasped! "What are Mr and Mrs Shinyshoes going to say when they come home? I squashed the flowers, sprayed water everywhere and there are lots of rabbits wandering around!"

"There's only one thing for it!" said Claude. "I'll have to go back out there."

"Into the *wilderness*?" said Sir Bobblysock. "Oh, Claude, you are brave."

"Actually," said Claude, "I rather like it!"

"Well, at least that makes one of us," said Sir Bobblysock.

Claude went to the
back door and looked out.
He gasped again!

"What is it now, Claude?"
called Sir Bobblysock.

"It's . . . it's . . . it's . . ."

". . . *lovely!*" said Claude.

"Well I never!" said
Sir Bobblysock.

The garden furniture was all nice and clean now that Claude had hosed it down. The birdbath was filled with water. The hose had been tidied away. And the rabbits had eaten all the grass!

"Thank you, rabbits!" said Claude.

"It's perfect," said Claude. "Well, *nearly* perfect.
I wish I hadn't squashed those flowers."

But Sir Bobblysock had noticed something else.
"Is that sandwich . . . *walking?*" he wondered.

"It's the ant!" chuckled Claude. "He just wanted a cucumber sandwich!"

"Well, I can't blame him," said Sir Bobblysock. "They are ever so nice."

Claude and Sir Bobblysock decided to stay outside and enjoy their picnic together.

"You know, Claude," said Sir Bobblysock, "I think I could get to like the wild life after all."

"Me too," said Claude. "Another cup of tea?"

"Oooh, yes *please*, Claude!" said Sir Bobblysock.

Later on, Claude was curled up in his bed at 112 Waggy Avenue when Mr and Mrs Shinyshoes returned home.

"Oh darling! What a surprise!" said Mr Shinyshoes. "You cleaned up the garden. The lawn's mown, the furniture's clean, the birdbath's full. You even squashed those horrible weeds."

"It wasn't me," said Mrs Shinyshoes. "Maybe Claude knows something about it."

"Don't be silly, dear," said Mr Shinyshoes.
"Claude's been fast asleep all day."

But Claude *did* know something about it. And we do too, don't we?

HODDER CHILDREN'S BOOKS

First published in Great Britain in 2020
by Hodder and Stoughton

1 3 5 7 9 10 8 6 4 2

Based on the original 'Claude' series
published by Hodder Children's Books,
written and illustrated by Alex T. Smith

Storybook text written by Davey Moore

Copyright in images and script for
It's a Jungle Out There written by Maria O'Loughlin
© 2020 Sixteen South Limited

A CIP catalogue record for this book
is available from the British Library.

ISBN 978 1 444 93863 0

Printed and bound in China

Hodder Children's Books
An imprint of Hachette Children's Group
Part of Hodder and Stoughton
Carmelite House
50 Victoria Embankment
London, EC4Y 0DZ

An Hachette UK Company
www.hachette.co.uk
www.hachettechildrens.co.uk

FSC
www.fsc.org
MIX
Paper from
responsible sources
FSC® C104740